This book belongs to

Ella Watson
....

sparkle town fairies

ROSIE
the
RUBY Fairy
and the Christmas Mail Mix-Up

Sarah Creese * Lara Ede

make
believe
ideas

In **Sparkle Town,** on Ruby Hill,
towering, tall, and proud,
there stood a bustling **Post Office**
with spires that reached the clouds.

Ruby Hill

POST
OFFICE

In **charge** of sorting all the mail,
each parcel, card, and letter,

SORTING ROOM

was **Rosie** the **Ruby Fairy** –
no one did it better!

With one swish of her ruby wand,
the mail was marked to go

by **Bee Express**
(for super fast)

Whoooooosh

Juno Jewel
1 Treasure Street
Sparkle Town

Buzzzzz

Flutter
Flutter

or **Butterfly**
(safe, but slow).

Daphne Diamond
The Diamond Boutique
Sparkle Town

Flutter
Flutter

Rosie liked to work at speed; her mail was **never** late.

At **Christmas** Rosie whizzed and dashed.
She had no time to pause.

Her **toughest** task was sorting all
the letters for **Santa Claus!**

This year the mail
was stacked
sky-high and,
in a ruby flurry,
she sent them off
by **turtle dove**,
marked:

**Cupcake Parlor —
PLEASE HURRY!**

Cupcake Parlor?
That's odd!
Christmas letters
usually go to the
North Pole.

Turtle Dove Christmas Delivery
No time to stop!

The next day Rosie got a call:

"**Cupcake Parlor** here. You sent the Christmas mail to us!"

Poor Rosie cried,

"OH, DEAR!"

"Whatever can I do?" she wailed.
"I used the **wrong address!**
And now the turtle doves are gone –
how will I fix this mess?"

Oh, no!

The turtle doves would **not** come back.

Are you sure you can't help?

Sorry, Madam, we're on vacation.

So she flew to ask the bees.

"We can't go to the North Pole, *brrzz* – our wings will surely freeze!"

Brrzz!

Next she searched
the fairy web
for someone else
to help . . .

Hmm.

I can do it!

but then
she suddenly realized:
"I'm fast, I'll go MYSELF!"

She grabbed the mail at super speed,
focused on her goal.
Then she took off on the journey
to **Santa, 1 North Pole.**

Good luck, Rosie!

Whooooosh

Whooooosh

Santa Claus
1 North Pole

Rosie **flew** in wind and snow,
with all her **flying force**.

Santa Claus
1 North Pole

But when she checked the map, she gasped, "Oh, no! I've flown **OFF COURSE!**"

"I **rushed** and got it wrong again," she cried out, feeling beat. "I've **ruined** Christmas," Rosie sobbed. But **then** came the pattering feet . . .

Santa Claus
1 North Pole

. . . of a **reindeer,** who smiled kindly
and said, "What can I do?"
She asked,
"Can you take me to Santa?"

Santa Claus
1 North Pole

He **nodded,** and off they flew.

Santa's house came into view,
and Rosie felt relieved.

Santa Claus
1 North Pole

She'd got there in the nick of time,
for today was **Christmas Eve!**

She knocked, and **Santa Claus** appeare

He said, "Dear, please come in."

"I hope I'm not too late," she said.

"Of course not; **let's begin!**"

CUPCAKE SPRINKLES

Santa Claus
1 North Pole

As Santa read each letter, the elves made gifts with care.

And Rosie soon fell fast asleep
in Santa's snug, soft chair.

The night's stars **twinkled** in the sky.
The sleigh was ready at last.
Santa said, "We'll take my reindeer —
I promise that they're **fast!**"

When the sleigh reached Sparkle Town, the fairies gave a **cheer**.
"Before I go," said Santa, "I have one last **idea**."

Hooray!

You made it, Rosie!

POST OFFICE

Hooray!

"Close your eyes
and hold my hand,
then wave
your wand,"
he said . . .

And, just like that, the sky was filled
with **FIREWORKS** of **ruby red!**

In the twinkling of a fairy's wand, Santa flew away.

And Rosie snuggled into bed, ready for **Christmas Day.**

Rosie learned that when you rush,
you can sometimes get in trouble.

But if you **try** and **don't give in**,
you can work through **any** muddle!